This book belongs to:

.................................................

.................................................

First e-book edition October 2021
First paperback edition October 2021

Story by Adam Groves
Illustrations by Katherine Turner

ISBN 9781739836917 (paperback)
ISBN 9781739836900 (ebook)

# Father Christmas and his Animal Crew

Written by Adam Groves

Illustrated by Katherine Turner

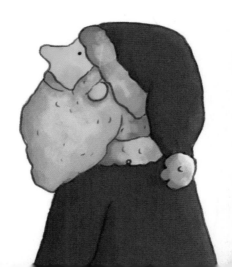

Father Christmas
had no time to spare
as he **rushed** to his
sleigh and took to the air.

"I'm in a great **hurry** to drop off your gifts before you wake up. I have to be **swift!**"

This is a tale of some **animal friends** who help **Father Christmas** before the night ends...

Whoosh went the sleigh through the starry sky
with a golden trail as the world **whizzed** by.

Packages, parcels, and boxes of toys -
all were delivered to the girls and boys.

As he flew over Britain
he hatched a **plan**.
"I need a **new** reindeer
to join the gang."

So he landed his sleigh in **London Zoo.**
"Have you a **reindeer** or caribou?"

"Ever so sorry," the zoo keeper said.
"Perhaps I can offer this lion instead?"

Father Christmas wasn't too sure.
He'd never flown with a **lion** before

but he couldn't see what else to do
so he attached the lion....

...and off they flew!

Whoosh went the sleigh
through the starry sky,
as the lion ROARED
and the world whizzed by.

Packages, parcels, and boxes of toys -
all were delivered to the girls and boys.

As he flew over **France** the sleigh lost speed.
"Another reindeer is what I need."

Before they crashed and came
to harm, he landed safely in a **farm**.

Father Christmas wasn't too sure.
He'd never flown with a **horse** before

but he couldn't see what else to do
so he attached the horse and off they **flew!**

Whoosh went the sleigh
through the starry sky
as the horse NEIGHED
and the world whizzed by.

Packages, parcels, and boxes of toys -
all were delivered to the girls and boys.

Next Father Christmas flew over India,
but the clouds were dark
and it grew ever windier.

The sleigh slowed
down to barely a trundle.
"We'll need to stop here
in the jungle."

Now Father Christmas
was getting **upset**.
"Has anyone a reindeer,
perhaps as a pet?"

"No!" said a girl, looking very **surprised**.
"Try an **elephant**," is what she advised.

Father Christmas wasn't too sure.

He'd **never** flown with
an **elephant** before

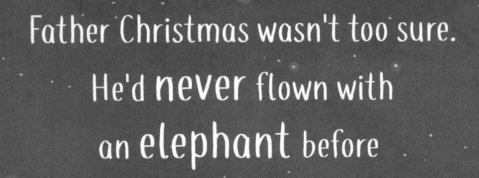

but he couldn't see
what else to do so he
attached the elephant
- and off they **flew!**

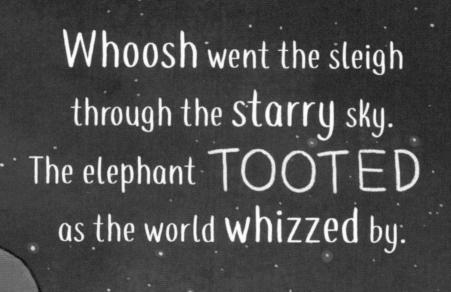

Whoosh went the sleigh
through the **starry** sky.
The elephant **TOOTED**
as the world **whizzed** by.

Packages, parcels,
and boxes of toys -
all were delivered
to the girls and boys.

Now they crossed a **Kenyan** plain
but the sleigh began to slow again.
"We'll have to take another break,"
he said, landing right beside a **lake**.

"There's **no reindeer** here,"
Father Christmas observed.

"We won't find one let alone a good herd."
Then out of the trees came a tall giraffe,
"Can I help?" he said with a nervous laugh.

Father Christmas wasn't too sure.
He'd never flown with a **giraffe** before

but he couldn't see
what else to do so
he attached the giraffe
– and off they flew!

Whoosh went the sleigh
through the starry sky.
The giraffe chuckled
and the world whizzed by.

Packages, parcels,
and boxes of toys –
all were delivered
to the girls and boys.

So when you give thanks this **Christmas time,**
remember the animals in this rhyme.

The lion, the horse, the elephant too
and the giggly giraffe who was part of the crew.

All of them had a role to play.
in delivering your presents this Christmas Day.

The End

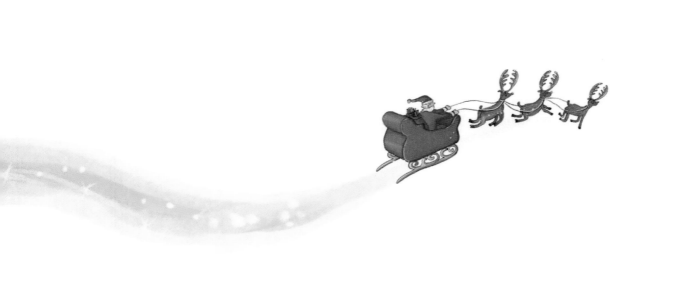
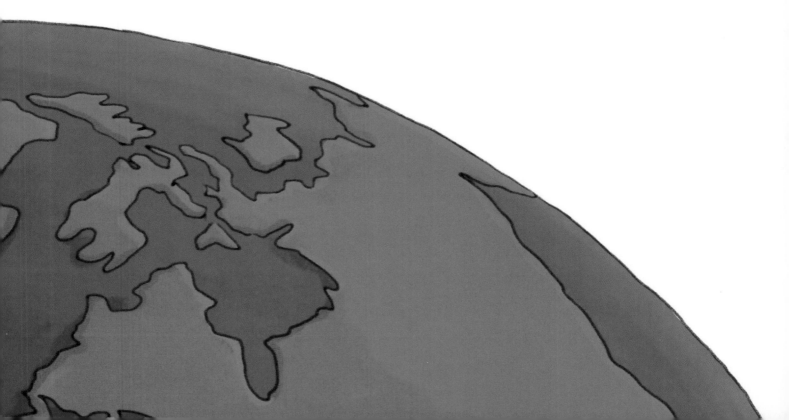

THIS IS ADAM GROVES'
FIRST CHILDREN'S BOOK. IT
WAS WRITTEN FOR, AND IS
DEDICATED TO, HIS SONS.

KATHERINE TURNER STUDIED FINE
ART AND HAS BEEN WORKING AS
A FREELANCE PAINTER AND
ILLUSTRATOR SINCE SHE
GRADUATED IN 2009. TO SEE MORE
OF HER WORK VISIT HER WEBSITE
OR HER INSTAGRAM PAGE.

www.ktdesigns.me

Instagram: kturnerdesigns

Printed in Great Britain
by Amazon